Little Red Tractor

A WHITE CHRISTMAS
ON
GOSLING FARM

By

Peter Tye

ISBN: 9781502377494

This story is from the original TV series. Four of the ten
stories were published by Scholastic, as Little Hippo
books,in 1999. I published them on kindle in 2012 and
as they were well received, published the other six.
In 2013, all the stories were published in paperback and
as they are independently published, they will only go out
of print if I want them to. The other major benefit is that
they are available, every hour, or very day   worldwide!

Peter Tye.

A WHITE CHRISTMAS ON GOSLING FARM

Stan opened one eye. Patch was sitting beside his bed,
wagging her tail. She pushed a wet cold nose into Stan's face.
"Oi! mumbled Stan, "that's enough of that!" but Patch nudged
him again..

"What ever's wrong with you this morning, Patch?" grumbled Stan. He sat up in bed. It seemed very bright outside; had he overslept?

He got out of bed and complained when his feet touched the floor. it seemed ever so cold.

He padded over to the window and drew back the curtains. The window was frosted up. He huffed on the frosty glass and rubbed a hole to peep through. "Oh dear, oh no!" he said, "you are right, Patch, there is something up - it's snowing!"

Stan gave Patch her breakfast and made some porridge and a mug of tea for himself.

After breakfast, Stan struggled into his warmest, winter overcoat. He wrapped a long green woolly scarf around his neck and pulled on his boots.

Then, after filling two buckets with steaming hot water, he opened the back door.

The door banged open and a howling wind swept snow into the kitchen!

"It's a real blizzard and no mistake!" shouted Stan, as he struggled through the doorway and set off across the yard.

The snow almost came over the top of Stan's boots!
But Patch thought it was great fun, as she charged through the deep soft snow.

The hens began to cackle as Stan pulled open the barn door. "Hello, Little Red Tractor!" he shouted. "Winter has arrived!"

Stan made up some warm mash for the chickens and took some into the stable for Jeremy the shire horse.

The he went back to the house for more hot water.

After several trips, Stan made six buckets filled with sloppy mash, which he loaded into Little Red Tractor's trailer, covering them with an old sheet of plywood.

"Hop in!" Stan shouted to Patch, as he climbed into Little Red tractor's cab. He turned the key and there was a splutter, a cough, and a noise which sounded as if Little Red Tractor was saying, "I don't think I want to go out in that weather." Then, Little Red Tractor's engine sprang into life, and after a few seconds to warm up, they drove out into the winter storm.

In Pig Field, snow was falling so thick and fast, Stan had a job to find the pig sties. But the pigs heard Little Red Tractor coming and began to squeal with excitement.

They knew breakfast was on its way. They tumbled out from their sties and charged through the snow towards Little Red Tractor.

Stan poured the mash, which was still hot, thanks to the old sheet of plywood, into the pig trough. Clouds of steam rose into the air as the pigs, squealing and grunting, greedily slurped their breakfast.

The next job for Stan, was to tend to the sheep.

Then after feeding and milking the cows he battled back through the yard towards the house. "Come on Patch!" he shouted, "it's time for a warm-up!"

The kitchen was warm and cosy. Patch stretched out by the oven as Stan made himself a mug of cocoa, which he was drinking when the 'phone rang.

It was Mrs Turvey, a neighbour at Blackthorn Cottage, who wondered if Stan could bring some milk and eggs across the fields, as all the lanes were blocked and she could not get to the shops. "I'm sure Little Red Tractor can make it, Mrs Turvey," said Stan. Now don't you worry, we'll be with you within the hour."

Stan put his overcoat, scarf and boots back on. The snow blew in again as he opened the back door and the wind seemed even stronger as he battled across the yard to Little Red Tractor's barn.

It was not long before Little Red Tractor's trailer was almost full. Stan had loaded two sacks of potatoes, a sack of flour, two churns of milk, a sack of carrots, several baskets filled with eggs, and a big box of farm churned butter. "It wouldn't do for Mrs Turvey to run out," he said to Patch, "not with all those young mouths to feed."

Stan filled the empty space with logs and tied a tarpaulin over the trailer to keep everything dry. He told Patch to stay and look after the farm and gave Little Red Tractor a pat on the bonnet. "Come on Little Red Tractor," he said. "We have a lot to do and a long way to go, so I think it will be a good idea to bolt on your snowplough.

With his snowplough fitted, Little Red Tractor set off across Middle Field and over the little bridge into Owl Wood Meadow.

Blackthorn Cottage, looked cosy and welcoming in the snow, and as Little Red Tractor stopped they were greeted by the Turvey children, who were jumping up and down with excitement.

Stan gave Mrs Turvey two dozen eggs - a big pat of butter and bags filled with carrots and potatoes. He also filled a bowl with flour and several jugs with milk.

Then he brought some logs in and stacked them by the fireplace.

"There you are Mrs Turvey," he said, "it wouldn't do for you to run out of logs, not in this weather.

Mrs Turvey thanked Stan and said that she did not know what they would do without good neighbours like him and Little Red Tractor.

Stan turned pink with embarrassment, told her she was very welcome but that they had more calls to make. He wanted to make sure everything was alright up at the windmill.

In Mill Lane, the snow was piled high in huge drifts and Little Red Tractor had to use his snowplough to get through.

Elsie and Stumpy were delighted to see Stan and little Red Tractor.

"I thought you might need a few things," said Stan, as he turned back the tarpaulin cover on Little Red Tractor's trailer.

"You're an angel, Stan," said Elsie.
For the second tome that day, Stan turned pink, but he covered his blushes by helping Stumpy carry logs and supplies into the house. Elsie wanted to make Stan a hot drink, he thanked her, but he had to get on, there were many more calls to make.

For the rest of the morning and into the afternoon, Stan and Little Red Tractor battled through the snow to visit all the cottages around Gosling Farm.

The last call was on Walter at the Garage. As Walter waved his thanks, Stan turned Little Red Tractor towards home. It had been snowing all day, but now they were heading into the full force of the blizzard.

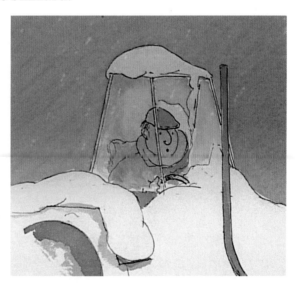

"Come on Little Red Tractor," urged Stan, "there's not far to go now." But even as he spoke, the snow was building up on Little Red Tractor's and windscreen.

The windscreen wipers were working very hard, but Stan found it difficult to see the side of the road.

He switched on the headlights, and was thinking how pretty the snowflakes looked as they swirled in the beam of light, when suddenly, there was something else!

A shadowy figure standing in the middle of the road, waving for him to stop!

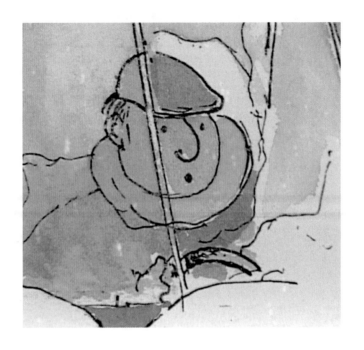

Stan slammed his foot on the brake pedal and Little Red
Tractor began to skid. "Oh no!" shouted Stan. "Stop Little Red

Tractor! Stop!"
But, Little Red Tractor could not stop and slithered off
towards the side of the road.

At last they shuddered to a halt, and the shadowy figure ran through the driving snow and peered into the cab.

"Are you alright, Stan?" It was Mr Jones from Beech Farm.
"Yes, I'm fine," said Stan, "but I'm not sure about Little Red Tractor.
He looks alright to me," said Mr Jones. "You're not in the ditch, the snowplough saved you."
 Mr Jones apologised. He had rushed out onto the road when he heard Little Red Tractor, because his enormous blue tractor, Big Fred, would not start and he was hoping Little Red Tractor would be able to lend some of his battery power to get Big Fred started.

Mr Jones walked behind, as Stan drove carefully around the corner to Beech Farm.

Big Fred stood at the end of the yard in a snowdrift, looking very sorry for himself.

Little Red Tractor set to work with his snow plough, to clear a space so that he could park next to Big Fred.Stan and Mr Jones joined the batteries together with electric cables.

"We're ready!" shouted Stan.

Mr Jones turned Big Fred's starter key, and with the power coming from Little Red Tractor's battery, Big Fred's engine began to turn - but very, very, slowly. Mr Jones shook his head."Come on little Red tractor!" shouted Stan, "you can do it! Little Red Tractor revved his engine as hard as he could, and Big Fred's engine began to turn faster and faster until, at last, it coughed and roared into life.

"Well done!" shouted Stan, as he took off the electric cables. "Come on Little Red Tractor, let's go home.

Mr Jones waved and Big Fred gave a hoot of thanks as Little Red Tractor drove out of Beech Farm.

Once again, they were heading into the full force of the blizzard and the howling wind seemed to be saying "You won't get home. I'm much too strong for a little tractor like you."

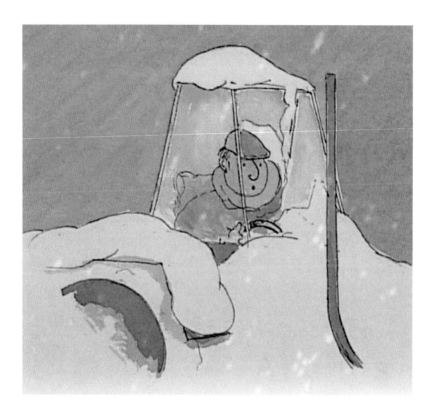

With his trailer slipping and sliding behind him, Little Red tractor pulled with all his might. But the wind would not give up. it found a way into the cabin and whistled around Stan's ears.

Stan began to feel, very, very cold. The wind blew harder and snow found its way through Little Red Tractor's radiator grill and by the time they were driving past Five oaks Field, his engine was beginning to splutter. "Come on Little Red Tractor!" urged Stan, "we're about to turn into our lane."Little Red Tractor struggled on, but with hardly enough power to push the snowplough through the deep snow drifts, it looked as if the wind was going to win.

"Don't give up!" shouted Stan, "I think I can see the farm!"At last, they turned into the shelter of the yard and Little Red Tractor's engine ran smoothly again. He tooted on his horn to Patch, who was very pleased to to see them arrive safely back on Gosling Farm.

Two days later, it was still very cold, but at least a wintry sun was shining. The snowploughs from Wrigglesworth were out clearing the roads, helped by Mr Jones and Big Fred, who was very pleased to be working again.

In the afternoon, Stan thought he heard Big Fred down by Whistling Bridge. "That's funny, Patch," he said. "I thought they cleared that stretch of road this morning."

Stan carried on working and did not see Big Fred turn into the lane to Gosling Farm, behind a stream of cars.

When the first car drove into the yard and hooted, Stan almost dropped the bale of straw he was carrying.It was Mrs Turvey, with all the children. "We've brought you a Christmas present!" they shouted.

"Oh my goodness!" said Stan. "It's Christmas Eve and I've forgotten to do my Christmas shopping!"

"We thought you might," said Mrs Turvey, "that's why the children and I made these for you." Mrs Turvey was carrying a big try of mince pies. "I don't know what to say," said Stan, "but thank you very much."

Another car drove into the yard. It was Stumpy and Elsie with a beautiful, home made Christmas Cake.

Stan hardly had time to thank them before more friends arrived with presents. Some were wrapped to go under the Christmas Tree, but others, like a Christmas Pudding, a box of dates and a bag full of tangerines, would go in the larder, ready for Christmas day.

Mr Jones drove up in Big Fred and handed Stan a plump turkey. "We all thought," he said, "that as you have been so busy looking after us and all your animals, that you won't have had time to do your own Christmas shopping."

Stan thanked everyone and was wishing them all a Merry Christmas, when Walter from the garage arrived. "I just want to say," said Walter, "that it was very kind of you and Little Red Tractor to help us out, and if it snows like that again, you may find these useful." Walter handed Stan two shiny new spot lights for Little Red Tractor.

On Christmas morning, it began to snow again. Stan wished the ducks a Merry Christmas as they flew over the farm on their way to the river. He fed all the animals, and wished them a Merry Christmas too.

Then, with everything taken care of, he went to the barn to put the shiny new spot lights on the front of Little Red Tractor's radiator. And, just for fun, he decorated them with holly.

"Merry Christmas Little Red Tractor," he said. "No more work for you today - you deserve a jolly good rest."

THE END

Made in United States
Orlando, FL
28 November 2021

10849686R00024